10 Minute Tales

D1150918

Timmy's Birthday

When you see these symbols:

Read aloud

Read aloud to your child.

Read alone

Support your child as they read alone.

Read along

Read along with your child.

EGMONT

We bring stories to life

Read aloud   Read along

It was a very special day at Nursery – Timmy's birthday! All his friends sang him a birthday song.

Paxton gave Timmy a card he had made. There was a picture of a beautiful birthday cake on the front.

Baah! Timmy was pleased. He loved birthday cake!

Read alone

Timmy and Paxton spread
jam on Timmy's birthday cake.

Read aloud   Read along

Harriet led the class outside.
They were going to have a birthday
party for Timmy!

Booh! Timmy bleated happily. Harriet
had set up a party table full of drinks
and sandwiches.

Ta-da! Harriet lifted the lid of the cake stand.
Timmy licked his lips. The cake looked so
tasty ... but it wasn't teatime yet!

Read alone

Outside, Harriet organised
a party for Timmy.

First, they played some party games.

Harriet turned on the music.
Timmy and his friends played
Musical Chairs.

When Harriet stopped the
music, poor Stripey didn't
have a chair! He was out of
the game, so he sat down on a
stump to watch his friends play.

Read alone

First, Timmy and his friends played Musical Chairs.

Read aloud   Read along

Harriet played the music again.
Timmy and his friends danced round
and round the cushions.

Then Timmy saw the party table in the yard.
He remembered his cake. It had looked so tasty ...

When the music stopped, Timmy's friends
each found a cushion. But Timmy couldn't
take his eyes off the cake. He was out
of the game!

Read alone

Timmy couldn't stop looking at
his cake, so he lost the game!

Read aloud   Read along

Timmy sat on a stump next to Stripey
and they watched their friends playing
the game.

But the thought of that yummy cake
was too much for Timmy. He wanted
some birthday cake – and he wanted it now!

When nobody was
watching, Timmy slipped
off his stump and
crept through
the gate.

Read alone

Timmy crept away from the party. He wanted to try the cake!

Read aloud **Read along**

Timmy tiptoed up to the cake stand. Oooh! He smelt the cake. Mmmm! Then he licked it. **Baah!** It tasted as good as it looked.

Timmy peered over his shoulder to check that nobody was watching. Yabba had won the game of Musical Chairs and was quacking loudly!

Timmy reached out, scooped up some jam and gobbled it happily. **Baah!**

Read alone

The cake tasted as good as it looked!

Suddenly, Harriet called everyone together for another game.

Cluck! Cluck!

Timmy put the lid back on so no one would know he had tasted the cake. Then he sneaked back to his friends.

Harriet was wearing a blindfold. She chased the friends around the garden, trying to find them by their voices. **Oink! Oink!**

Mee-eew! Quack!

No one noticed that Timmy had been missing!

Read alone

Timmy went back to play with his friends.

Read aloud   **Read along**

Timmy couldn't stop thinking about the cake. He wanted more! His friends were busy trying to run away from Harriet, so they didn't see him sneak back to the party table.

Timmy lifted the lid, licked his lips ... and ate every last piece of his birthday cake!

But Timmy wanted more cake.
He ate it all by himself!

Read aloud   Read along

After Paxton had won the game,
Harriet took off her blindfold. It was
time for Timmy's birthday tea!

Harriet led the excited friends to the
party table. They couldn't wait to
taste Timmy's birthday cake!

But where was Timmy?

It was time for tea.
But where was Timmy?

Harriet waited by the cake stand. Surely Timmy would come if he knew it was time for his birthday cake?

Ta-da! Harriet lifted the lid of the cake stand but ... oh dear! It had been eaten up! All that was left was a sticky crumb and a blob of icing.

Read alone

Timmy's cake had been eaten!

Read aloud   Read along

Before Harriet could ask the class
who had eaten the cake, she heard
a funny noise.

BUUUURRRRPPPP!

Harriet peered under the table. There was Timmy,
holding his tummy. He felt very sick from eating
too much cake!

Harriet couldn't believe
he had eaten it all.
Neither could Timmy.

Read alone

Timmy was under the table.
He felt sick from eating too much.

Timmy crawled out from under the table
and looked at his friends. They were sad
not to have any birthday cake to eat.

Booh! Timmy felt bad for eating all of the cake.

Harriet gave Timmy a dustpan and brush, and
he swept up the crumbs.

Suddenly, Timmy had a brilliant idea. He would
make a new cake for his friends to say sorry.

Read alone

But then Timmy had an idea.
He would make a new cake!

Timmy hurried back into the Nursery. He found all the things that Harriet used for making birthday cakes.

He poured jam on the sponge and squirted icing on top. Then he decorated the cake with lots of tasty fruit.

Timmy was very proud! He ran outside to share the new birthday cake with his friends.

Timmy put lots of icing on the new birthday cake.

Read aloud   Read along

Timmy placed his cake on the table
and lifted the lid. Ta-da!

Mittens mewed in disgust. Mee-eew!
This was not the beautiful cake they had made.
This was a sticky, fruity mess!

But Yabba didn't mind. She gave Timmy's cake
a sniff. Then a lick. Quack! It was very tasty!

Soon the friends were
all sharing the cake.
All, that is, except
Timmy. He'd had enough
birthday cake for
one day!

Read alone

The friends shared the tasty cake.
Well done, Timmy!

Timmy Time

Congratulations to Alexander!

In December 2010 we ran a competition on www.egmont.co.uk, challenging fans to create a Timmy Time birthday card or cake.

The winning entry is published here (well done Alexander!) and our runners-up can be viewed online at www.egmont.co.uk.

Thank you to everyone who entered!

Plus! Enjoy more books from the 10 Minute Tale range...

10 Minute Adventures

Visit www.egmont.co.uk/10minutetales
for exciting puzzles, games and activities!

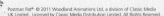